Ready, Set, GO!

Story and pictures by
John Stadler

HarperTrophy®
A Division of HarperCollins Publishers

HarperCollins®, ☕®, Harper Trophy®, and I Can Read Book®
are trademarks of HarperCollins Publishers Inc.

Ready, Set, Go!
Copyright © 1996 by John Stadler
Printed in the U.S.A. All rights reserved.

Library of Congress Cataloging-in-Publication Data
Stadler, John.
  Ready, set, go! / story and pictures by John Stadler.
    p.   cm. — (An I can read book)
  Summary: When she plays with bigger dogs, Sasha proves herself and her
abilities.
  ISBN 0-06-024944-7. — ISBN 0-06-024947-1 (lib. bdg.)
  ISBN 0-06-444238-1 (pbk.)
  [1. Dogs—Fiction. 2. Competition (Psychology)—Fiction.]   I. Title.
II. Series.
PZ7.S77575Re   1996   95-26452
[E]—dc20   CIP
                                                                   AC

Typography by Nancy Sabato
❖
First Harper Trophy edition, 1998

Visit us on the World Wide Web!
http://www.harperchildrens.com

To my great dog Sasha

(and to her big cousin up the hill)

Sasha went to visit

her cousin Oliver.

"Hello, Oliver," she said.

"Hello to you,

little cousin,"

said Oliver.

"Do you want to play

with me?" asked Sasha.

"Play with you?"

said Oliver.

"You are too little

to play with."

"But Oliver," Sasha said,

"I am not a baby anymore.

I am almost as big as you.

I can ride a bike.

I can go to the store."

"I even won first prize

in a skating race," said Sasha.

"Who cares about prizes?"

said Oliver.

"I am waiting to play with Juliet."

Then Oliver said,

"Let's have a contest

while I wait for her.

We can build snowmen,

and then we'll see

who is big and who is not.

Ready, set, go!"

"Look at mine,"

Sasha said.

"Mine is better,"

Oliver shouted.

"I am the best!"

"Now let's build forts
and have a snowball fight,"
Oliver said. "Ready, set, go!"

12

Sasha started.

"I win!" Oliver cried.

"I am the greatest."

"I am going skating now!"

Sasha said.

"Fine," said Oliver.

"Here comes Juliet."

"We could all skate together,"
said Sasha.

"You're cute, Sasha," Juliet said,
"but you are too little
to play with us."

"Come on, Juliet," said Oliver,
"let's build snowmen."

17

"Look, mine is better than ever!"
Oliver shouted.

"Nice try," said Juliet,

"but I win!

I am the greatest!"

19

"Let's try something different,"

Oliver said.

"Okay," said Juliet.

"Let's have a snowball fight."

"I have the biggest snowball
in the world," Oliver said.

BOOM!

"No one can beat me,"

said Juliet.

"Oh yeah?" Oliver said.

"Sasha won a prize for skating.

Have a race with her."

"Little Sasha?" said Juliet.

"Are you afraid?" asked Oliver.

"I am fast," Sasha said.

"All right," said Juliet,

"but you will see."

"Your baby skates are no match
for my rocket skates,"
said Juliet.
"Ready, set, go!"
Oliver shouted.

The race began.

"Help!" Juliet cried.

"Something is wrong

with my skates!"

She flew up into the air.

"Catch me!" Juliet cried.

"No way," said Oliver.

"I will catch you,"
Sasha said.

"Look out!"
Oliver shouted.

CRASH!

"Little Sasha is great!"

said Juliet.

"She saved me!"

"Of course she's great," said Oliver.

"She is my cousin."

"Sasha, let's play some more,"
said Juliet.

"Play with you?" said Sasha.

"Come on," said Oliver.

"Well, all right," Sasha said,

"but get ready—

you haven't seen anything yet!"